Mattie Mae

Mattie Mae

Edna Beiler

Illustrated by Esther Rose Graber

Second Edition

Herald
Press

Scottdale, Pennsylvania
Waterloo, Ontario

Library of Congress Cataloging-in-Publication Data
Beiler, Edna.
    Mattie Mae / Edna Beiler ; illustrated by Esther Rose Graber.—2nd
    ed.
            p. cm.
    Summary: The problems and pleasures of an eight-year-old
    Amish girl who lives with her family in Virginia.
        ISBN 0-8361-9143-2 (alk. paper)
        [1. Amish—Fiction.   2. Family life—Virginia—Fiction.]   I. Graber,
    Esther Rose, ill.   II. Title.

PZ7.B388235 Mat 2000
[Fic]—dc21

                                                                    99-058469

The paper used in this publication is recycled and meets the mini-
mum requirements of American National Standard for Information
Sciences—Permanence of Paper for Printed Library Materials,
ANSI Z39.48-1984.

MATTIE MAE
Copyright © 1967, 2000 by Herald Press, Scottdale, Pa. 15683
        Published simultaneously in Canada by Herald Press,
        Waterloo, Ont. N2L 6H7. All rights reserved
Library of Congress Catalog Card Number: 99-058469
International Standard Book Number: 0-8361-9141-2
Printed in the United States of America
Cover art by Joy Dunn Keenan

09 08 07 06 05 04 03 02 01 00 10 9 8 7 6 5 4 3 2 1

Over 20,000 copies in print in all editions
To order or request information, please call
1-800-759-4447 (individuals); 1-800-245-7894 (trade).
Website: www.mph.org

To Uncle Noah

Contents

Foreword

When I was a little girl, I lived in a place in southern Virginia much like the one described in these stories. Several years ago, I stopped there for a brief visit.

The farm where I had lived is now a housing project. The farmhouse just across the road from it is (of all things!) the headquarters for a country club. Where the catalpa grove once sprawled, the tangled growth of honeysuckle vines has given way to neat green lawns, clipped close.

In fact, that whole area is an enormous suburb, from the city of Norfolk to the sea. I suppose even Dismal Swamp (that darkest mystery of my childhood) is being drained and farmed in neat and tidy fields. It is all very sad.

I am glad that a little of that past can be preserved in these stories. However, this book is not history in any other sense of the word. I have tried to remain true to that countryside, as I remember it. But the incidents in the stories are not necessarily true happenings.

The cousins I played with as a child are not the cousins that Mattie Mae knows, nor are the uncles, aunts, assorted relatives, and neighbors in these stories identified with real people.

There is one exception. The Uncle Tobe of these stories was a real uncle who gladdened my childhood by his visits and saddened us all by his death. He is the Uncle Noah to whom this book is dedicated.

—*Edna Beiler*

Preface

The character of Mattie Mae came to me from many sources. She is a combination of ideas picked up from stories my mother told about her childhood, and memories from my own childhood, plus events that are purely imaginary.

However, I did try to recapture a time and a place that are gone forever. For this, I gathered authentic details. The tide of urbanization has all but obliterated the country setting where these stories are supposed to have taken place. So I sought to recapture that time and that place in stories, where the scenes cannot be easily erased.

In these stories, I have tried to stay away from easy and shallow moralizing. Instead, the stories have their basis in enduring values such as respect for others, understanding for those who are different, and getting along together in families and neighborhoods.

Above all, these stories are to be enjoyed. They are

gifts to all the boys and girls who spend their spare minutes curled up in odd positions on chairs or on the floor, with their noses perpetually in books!

—*Edna Beiler*

Here Comes Mattie Mae!

But, Mom!" Mattie Mae wailed as she plunked her schoolbooks on a chair. "Today was library day at school, and I got a new book. I wanted to read—"

"I'm sorry, but Hannah Snavely needs this money," Mom said. "Her mother's come to live with her, and they need every cent they can scrape together, I'm sure."

"Why can't Becky go?" Mattie Mae demanded. Becky was her next-older sister.

"She has to help Malinda with the chores. Ellie's in town taking orders for market day, and Henry and Pop are helping Uncle Yonie butcher and won't be back till late."

"*Ach* (oh), my! Maybe Lizbet could—" Lizbet was Mattie Mae's next-younger sister.

"No!" Mom sounded as if she really meant what she

said. "She's too little to walk down there by herself. And on such a cold day!"

Benjy, Mattie Mae's little brother, came trotting up. "I want to go! Take me along, Mattie Mae!"

Mom shook her head. "Your legs would be tired long before you got home, Benjy. Bundle up good, Mattie Mae. It's really cold."

Mattie Mae pulled on her warm cloak with a sigh and tied her bonnet under her chin. She put the money in one hand and slipped her mitten on over it.

She didn't want to tramp all that way over to Snavely's to pay Hannah the money Mom owed her for a sewing job. Not on such a cold day, anyway. Not with her library book, *Heidi,* waiting to be read.

I think it's real mean of Mom to make me do it, Mattie Mae thought as she stomped out. She would have slammed the door, but she knew Mom would make her come back and close it right!

Mattie Mae usually didn't mind skipping up to Perry's Corners. She took the shortcut through the fields, along the bank of the big ditch. It drained their farm and Uncle Alvin's and Uncle Yonie's and all the other farms around. In that flat country, land couldn't drain itself.

When the ditch gurgled along beside her, full of water, Mattie Mae liked to toss wood chips into it. She would think of them bobbing along, all the way out to the ocean, twenty-five miles away.

Today was different. It was cold and wet, so Mattie Mae had to walk along the highway. Today she wanted to stay home and read *Heidi.*

By the time Mattie Mae got to Hannah's house, her nose was blue from cold, and her feet felt like lumps of ice. She knocked on the door. Somebody said, "Come in!" It didn't sound like Hannah's voice. *That must be Mammy Snavely,* Mattie Mae thought.

She stepped inside. The room was so dark that at first she couldn't see anything. After her eyes adjusted to the shadows, she saw a dim figure sitting beside the stove, in a rocking chair.

"How—how are you, Mammy?" Mattie Mae asked.

"So-so. Not bad for an old woman like me!" Mammy Snavely said.

Mattie Mae went closer. My—she was the *oldest* woman Mattie Mae had ever seen! And she was sitting there knitting.

"Isn't it too dark for you to see to knit?" Mattie Mae asked.

Mammy threw her head back and laughed. Mattie Mae liked the deep wrinkles running from her eyes and down toward her chin. They looked as if she laughed a lot.

"Dark or light—it's all the same to me," Mammy said. "You see, I'm blind, but I can knit anyway. Now, suppose you tell me who you are?"

"I'm Dan Miller's little girl, Mattie Mae."

Mammy nodded her head. "The Amish family where Hannah works. Yes. I remember."

"That's right. And Mom owed Hannah some money, so she sent me down with it."

"How old are you, Mattie Mae?" Mammy Snavely asked. "You sound young-like."

"Ach, I'm not so little. I'm eight already," Mattie Mae said.

Just then, Hannah came bursting in. "Why, Mammy—and Mattie Mae! How are you, Baby?"

Mattie Mae mumbled something. She could feel her face get red. She always felt funny when Hannah called her Baby. After all, Lizbet and Benjy were both younger than she was!

"Mom sent me with your money," Mattie Mae finally said.

16

"There, Mammy! See what I told you!" Hannah's face beamed. "She's the nicest woman I ever worked for. Just think, sendin' somebody all this way on a chilly day like this. Baby, you've got to get warm before you go back."

Hannah bustled around some. Her house was tiny and plain, even plainer than Mattie Mae's own Amish house. Everything was neat and clean, though.

Just like Hannah herself, Mattie Mae thought.

By then, she was settled close to the stove with her feet on the wide shelf that stuck out at one end. Hannah gave her something to drink. Mattie Mae didn't know what it was, but it was hot and spicy and made her feel good all over.

She got up as she took the last sip. "I'll have to go. Mom didn't say I could stay," she said.

"I 'spect you'd better. It's gettin' dark rather fast,"

Hannah said. "Tell your mom, 'Thank you kindly for sendin' the money.' "

Mattie Mae skipped down the road toward home. She was careful about cars. Mom had told her that so often!

Just the same, she was thinking. Thinking about Hannah and Mammy Snavely. And about Mom, too.

"The nicest woman I ever worked for." That's what Hannah had said about her mom.

Mom knew it wouldn't hurt me to walk down here. So she wasn't really mean *to make me come,* Mattie Mae thought.

The wind was sharp in her face, so she turned and walked backward for a bit. She could see all the way back to Perry's Store. Yes, that was Hannah now, coming out with a bag in her arms.

Mattie Mae's family wasn't rich. They often had to do without things, but there was always plenty to eat at home. Canned or dried or pickled. Food Pop and Mom bought at the store or leftovers from the trip to market. Food everywhere, it sometimes seemed.

What would it feel like to be so poor that we had to go hungry sometimes? she wondered.

A few minutes later, Mattie Mae burst into the Miller kitchen. "Oh, Mom," she said, "Mammy Snavely's blind! Did you know that? But she can knit, anyway. And, Mom—"

Mattie Mae had to stop for breath. She pulled off her cloak and tossed it on the woodbox.

"Mom—could I go and read to her sometimes? Do you think she'd want me to?"

Mom nodded her head. "Ach, yes. She'd like that. And you read real good for your age, Mattie Mae. I'll hunt up that old shawl of mine. It's faded but soft and warm. There's wool Grandmom gave me that I've never had time to use. She can knit it up for me. I'll be glad to pay her—"

"And I'll be glad to take the money over anytime," Mattie Mae said.

The fire felt good against her cold cheeks. The whole kitchen felt warm and nice, with *Heidi* lying there, waiting to be read. Best of all, Mattie Mae felt good inside, too, as she picked up *Heidi* and began to read.

Hello, Uncle Tobe

"Come on—tell another story!" Lizbet, Mattie Mae's littlest sister, said.

Mom shook her head at her. "Uncle Tobe's tired. He just got here today. Don't be such a *beggar's bag.*"

Mattie Mae was glad she hadn't said anything. She didn't want to have Mom call *her* a beggar's bag. But she did hope Uncle Tobe would tell some more stories.

Lizbet leaned against his knee. Benjy bounced up and down on his lap every time the story turned exciting. Even eleven-year-old Becky sat nearby, while Mattie Mae got as close to him as she could.

"Uncle Tobe's tired," Mom said firmly. "It's time for you children to be in bed, anyway. Now, scoot—right away."

"But, Mom," Mattie Mae began. "Tomorrow's Saturday—"

"Don't you be a beggar's bag, too!" Mom said to her.

"But Becky gets to stay up," Mattie Mae muttered under her breath.

It seemed to her that Becky had the best of everything. When company came, she could stay up until Mom and Pop went to bed. She could help Malinda and Ellie and Mom with grown-up work like baking cakes and scrubbing the kitchen.

Mattie Mae always had to do little bitty baby chores that even Benjy could do, like carrying wood or doing the dishes.

"There'll be lots of time for you to talk to Uncle Tobe. He's staying a month or so," Mom said kindly.

Mattie Mae didn't pay any attention to her. She stomped upstairs as hard as she dared and snapped at poor Lizbet for being so slow.

The next morning, Mom didn't go to the Saturday market because Uncle Tobe was visiting us. Usually she and Pop left early in the morning—long before daylight. On the market wagon, they would bump into town behind their trotting Prince. The iron-rimmed wagon wheels jolted along on the rough road and shook them up.

Pop rented a spot at the roofed open-air market, backed their wagon in, and sold produce off the back of the wagon. They were at the market all day.

This Saturday, Mom stayed home to get Uncle Tobe's breakfast because he was company.

"I ought to go over to see Grandpop this morning," Uncle Tobe said. "Do you have a horse to spare, Lizzie?"

Mattie Mae thought it sounded funny for Mom to be called Lizzie, but lots of things were different when Uncle Tobe came to visit. He lived in Indiana, where Mom and Pop and Grandpop and—well, everybody—used to live. That was a long time ago, before Mattie Mae was born.

Pop had told her how they heard about this farmland in southern Virginia. Farms were hard to buy in Indiana, so they decided to move. Uncle Tobe stayed behind, but every year he came to visit them.

"You can take Belle and the single buggy," Mom said.

"You'd better have somebody show you the way," Malinda put in.

Right away, Becky sat up straight. "I know how to get there," she said. "Go down to Perry's Corners, then turn left. After you cross the big highway, it's the second lane to the right. Not so?"

Becky looked at Mom, and she nodded. Mattie Mae looked down at her plate. A lump came into her throat.

She liked going to Grandpop's more than anything else. She had cousins scattered all around, all from Amish families like her own. The one she liked best was Cousin Lizbet, who lived right in the same yard with Grandpop. Of course, Becky would get to go. Becky always got to do everything.

"I'm sorry, Becky," Mom said firmly. "I need you to help with the Saturday work today."

Uncle Tobe looked at Mattie Mae. "How about you? Do you know the way? I wouldn't want to end up out at Virginia Beach, you know."

"Ach, my—yes!" Mattie Mae said in a tight voice. "The house with the stone lion in the yard—that's the one. I know I can find it." Grandpop's house had a stone lion because it had been a big plantation house once upon a time.

"I think Mattie Mae will do just fine if she doesn't talk your left ear off on the way," Mom said. "Run up and get a clean apron, Mattie Mae."

Mattie Mae dashed upstairs. She couldn't find a clean apron of her own, so she borrowed one of Becky's. It was way too big for her, of course. It had a three-cornered rip in it that Mom had not mended the week before.

"She's all right," Uncle Tobe said when Mom frowned. "Just like you at her age, Lizzie."

"Now, bundle up good. That wind is cold," Mom said.

She buttoned Mattie Mae's cape and tied Uncle Tobe's scarf for him.

"You're making a baby out of me," Uncle Tobe said.

"Well, you don't have a wife to look out for you, and somebody has to," Mom told him with a laugh.

Uncle Tobe laughed, too. Then he brought Belle and the buggy around, and Mattie Mae got in. She waved good-bye to Becky, who was filling the scrub bucket, getting ready to scrub the kitchen floor.

In some ways, things are evened up, after all, Mattie Mae decided. *Becky doesn't have everything just the way she wants, either.*

Belle went *clop-clop-clopping* down the road. She turned her head to one side and blew a riffle of foam from her mouth.

Mom wasn't around to call Mattie Mae a beggar's bag. So she said, "Tell another story, Uncle Tobe," and settled herself to listen.

A Box for Benjy

"Mom! I wanta get up!" Benjy wailed for the tenth time in ten minutes.

"Yes, I know you want to get up, Benjy, but you can't," Mom told him. "The doctor said you have to stay in bed—remember? Right in bed until your fever goes down."

"But I'm not sick, Mom. I don't feel a single bit sick. I wanta get up right now."

"Mattie Mae, you run in and play with him for a while," Mom said. "I've got to scrub these potatoes to cook or we'll never have dinner today."

With only a little sigh, Mattie Mae put away her paper dolls. She did feel sorry for Benjy. *It must be awful to have to stay in bed when you don't feel sick!*

"What shall we play?" she asked Benjy.

Benjy tossed around on the pillow. "Don't wanta

play anything. Wanta get up," he repeated.

Mattie Mae curled herself up on the foot end of his bed. "Why don't we play our pretend game? You know, the one Aunt Mattie taught us."

Benjy screwed up his mouth. At first Mattie Mae thought it wouldn't work.

Then he said, "I wish Aunt Mattie would come to visit us again."

"Ach, so do I," Mattie Mae agreed. "Mom's written to her that you're sick, so maybe she will. But we can play her game anyway, can't we?"

"I guess so," Benjy agreed.

He lay back on his pillow and screwed his eyes tight shut. Mattie Mae leaned her head on her arm and pasted her eyes tight shut.

"Ready?" she asked softly.

"Yes."

"You go first, Benjy. What do you see?"

"I see the swamp way, way back at the edge of our farm," Benjy said.

Mattie Mae opened her eyes for a minute, she was so surprised. "You're supposed to see something pretty, not an old tangle like that, Benjy."

"It is pretty, the way I see it," Benjy insisted. "You're not to interrupt like that, either. That's Aunt Mattie's rule!"

"All right. Go on," Mattie Mae said meekly.

"And growing right in all that tangle of green stuff, I see the most gorgeous flowers," Benjy said.

28

Mattie Mae had to hide a grin. Benjy liked to use all the big long words he could pick up. She wondered where he had heard *gorgeous*.

"They're as big as plates, the kind Mom uses for the bread."

"What color are they, Benjy?" Mattie Mae was getting interested, too.

"All colors. Some are red with blue speckles on them—blue, like the color of the robin's eggs in the nest hanging in the lilac bush. Some are orange with green speckles on them. Some are purple with white speckles. An'—ach, just every color you can think of. And when the sun shines on them, they shine right back at the sun."

Mattie Mae, with her eyes still tight shut, was "seeing" the flowers Benjy had described, each separate one as he told about it. When he came to the part "when the sun shines on them, they shine right back," it seemed as if all the flowers she had imagined were shining at the same time.

"Was that a good one, Mattie Mae?" Benjy asked.

"Ach, yes. I liked it a lot. Now it's my turn. And I'm seeing the catalpa grove, Benjy. Not the way it is now, but the way it will be later, when the honeysuckle vines make such a sweet smell all over it. I'm creeping along under the vines, sniffing as I go. And now—what do you think I see, Benjy?"

Benjy gave a happy little jerk in bed. "Ach, what is it? Tell me quick, Mattie Mae!"

"A bunny nest. I see the mom bunny go hoppity, hoppity, hoppity along a little trail she has through the weeds. Then I scrape away the leaves and stuff and find four little baby bunnies. Oh, they feel so soft, Benjy. I can feel them, too."

Benjy gave a long sigh. "If only we could find a nest like that this summer."

"Wait! I'm not finished," Mattie Mae told him. "After I've looked at the bunnies and held them in my hands, I put them back in their nest and push leaves over them just the way mom bunny had fixed it. Then I crawl away backward until I'm out of sight. But I don't go away. Oh, no!"

Benjy leaned forward. He forgot to keep his eyes shut, he was so excited. "Then what, Mattie Mae?"

"I wait and wait so long that I feel little prickles go up and down my legs the way they do when you sit still a long time. When I'm just about to give up and go home, I see the momma bunny come hippity hopping back again."

"Ach, yes," Benjy said. "And she hops right into the nest with her babies. And then you crawl away without making a bit of noise, so you won't scare her again."

Mattie Mae opened her eyes, too. She laughed. "Whose pretend picture is this, anyway?" she asked.

Benjy could tell she was teasing, though. He laughed, too.

"Let's do it again," he urged.

Before they started, Becky came rushing in, bring-

ing a lot of cool air along with her.

"Ach, my, but it's been a chilly April," she said. "Here's the mail, Mom."

"Yes, it has been cold for April, here in Virginia," Mom said. "I wonder how the others are getting along at the market."

Mom usually went along to market on Saturday, but today she stayed home because Benjy was in bed. Mattie Mae's oldest sister, Malinda, had gone with Pop instead. Henry and Ellie always delivered the things people had ordered, going right to their houses.

"Come on, Mom," Becky said. "Open the mail. There's a package—why, it's for Benjy. See, here's your name—Benjy. It's from Aunt Mattie."

Mom dropped her work. "There's a card here, too," she said. "Aunt Mattie says she's sorry she can't come, so she's sending you something instead."

Benjy took the scissors Becky gave him and snipped the strings. By then, Lizbet had showed up, too.

"Ooooh!" they all said as Benjy pulled the package open.

Inside was a box. There were so many things in it that Mattie Mae's head nearly spun, just looking. She saw scissors, crayons, paper (white and all kinds of pretty colors, like red and purple and blue), a scrapbook, several jars of paste all carefully wrapped in cloth so they wouldn't break, coloring books, pencils, and a big pack of pictures that Aunt Mattie had cut out of magazines.

"There's a little package in the bottom—no, two of them!" Lizbet said. "Look."

"This one has *your* name on it," Becky told her. "And this is for you, Mattie Mae."

Mattie Mae took her package. "To my namesake, Mattie Mae," Aunt Mattie had written on the outside.

She pulled off the brown paper just as Lizbet did the same thing to hers.

"Oh, Mom! Look!" they both screamed at the same time.

"Ach, now, why did Aunt Mattie bother with that? You girls aren't sick," Mom said.

Mattie Mae could tell she was teasing. She didn't really listen, though, because she was so busy looking at her present—a rag doll! She had a flat face with a long, thin neck. And she wore Amish clothes, just like Mattie Mae's clothing, a blue dress with a long pinafore apron of white organdy over it.

"What are these funny, flat things in the bottom of

the box?" Benjy asked.

Mom looked at them closely. "Those are for the girls, too. They're made of cardboard and covered with oilcloth. If I sew them together, they'll each have a little satchel to go with their doll babies."

"I'm going to name mine Christine," Lizbet said. That was Lizbet's favorite name. She was always wishing she had Christine for a name instead of her own.

"What are you going to call yours, Mattie Mae?" Becky asked, with a gleam in her eyes.

Mattie Mae knew why she was asking. She had named all of her dolls Alice, but till now she never had more than one at a time, so she couldn't see that it mattered. Even so, the rest of the family always teased her about it, as Becky was doing now.

"Don't do that, Becky," Mom said sharply.

Becky quit grinning and went out to the kitchen. Mattie Mae had already made up her mind.

"I'd like to sew some more clothes for Alice, Mom. May I?" she asked.

"Me, too!" Lizbet jumped up. "I want to sew, too, Mom."

"All right. And what are *you* going to do, Benjy boy?"

They all looked at Benjy. He sat in his bed, smiling to himself. He had a white sheet of paper on his lap and was holding a red crayon in one hand.

"I'm going to make those flowers I saw in my pretend picture. That's what I'm going to do," he declared.

Something to Tell Your Children

Mattie Mae closed her book with a sigh. She got up from Mom's rocking chair and went out to the kitchen.

"Do you have your Saturday chores all done?" Malinda asked. "Mom will be home any time now."

"Ach, yes. I finished those long ago." Mattie Mae sat on the edge of the woodbox and looked around at the clean kitchen. "I'm tired of rain, Malinda."

It was a rainy spring day. For weeks it had rained and rained and rained. The drainage ditches were full and overflowing. Some of Pop's fields were like lakes.

It wasn't so bad on weekdays, when Mattie Mae was in school. But on Saturday, she wanted to go outside and play!

"I know," Malinda said. She inched a loaf of bread out of the oven and began to rub lard on the top with a little rag. "But I think it has stopped now. Maybe the sun will come out."

"I hope so." Mattie Mae went to the window and looked out. She stopped to squint through the one funny pane that made the lawn seem to slope up, although it was perfectly flat.

"If it clears off, I want you to go over to Uncle Yonie's place," Malinda told her.

Mattie Mae nodded and leaned against the window, but she didn't see even a peep of sunlight.

"Mom said we should take a loaf of this bread over to Aunt Amanda," Malinda said. "She isn't able to bake right now, and they're so tired of store bread. Oh, yes, Mom wants to send back a pint of vinegar to replace what she borrowed last week, too."

Mattie Mae wasn't really listening. She turned away from the window and leaned against the sink. "Why don't we ever have any adventures, like they do in books?" she asked.

Malinda lined up her loaves of bread and stretched a snow-white tea towel over them.

"What kind of adventure?"

"Ach, you know. Any kind." Mattie Mae creased her forehead into a frown. "Even the kind Pop and Uncle Yonie were telling about last evening."

"Getting caught in a blizzard sounds exciting when you talk about it afterward," Malinda said. "I'm just as glad I don't have those kinds of adventures, thank you."

Mattie Mae didn't quite believe her big sister. Here it was at the end of a rainy Saturday afternoon. Mom and Ellie would soon be coming home on the bus. That was nice to think about, but it happened every week. A long time later, Pop and Henry would come bumping home in the market wagon, pulled by Prince. Then they'd all go to bed.

Mattie Mae liked to read, but now she wished something would happen. Something different. A real adventure.

"The sun is coming out," Malinda said. "Now, put your school cape on, Mattie Mae. Mom wanted us for sure to send those things over to Aunt Amanda if we could."

"All right," Mattie Mae agreed, "but it won't be anything to tell my children about."

She didn't think how that sounded until Malinda began to laugh. She laughed so hard that Mattie Mae couldn't help laughing, too.

"I'm sorry, Mattie Mae," Malinda gasped. "But I wouldn't worry about that for a while yet. There's plenty of time for things to happen before you grow up."

She helped Mattie Mae button her cape and don her bonnet. Then she handed her the loaf of bread, wrapped in a towel, and a little bottle of vinegar.

"Wear your rubber boots!" she called after Mattie Mae.

Sometimes Malinda can be as fussy as Mom about things like that, Mattie Mae thought.

The outdoors looked shiny wet in the sunshine. The grass was dark green. Water dripped from the porch eaves and stood in puddles everywhere.

Mattie Mae skipped down the back lane, humming to herself. She waved to Benjy and Lizbet, who were playing in the barn loft. She felt alive, even if she wasn't having any adventures.

It wasn't until she was past the oats field, almost to

the line fence, that she thought of the big ditch. If she went around by the road, she could cross it on the big bridge. But here at the end of the lane, there was only a narrow plank.

During the summer, the plank didn't seem scary. She would just take a run and hop across. Then the ditch was empty. But not now! The other ditches all emptied into this one—the big ditch that went out to the ocean.

Mattie Mae walked on slowly. The plank looked slippery, and the water burbled along just under it. But she didn't want to go back, all that long way, to the house and around by the road. And she couldn't cut across the flooded fields. She would stick in the mud, or the water would be too deep.

I guess I'll try the plank, she decided.

Mattie Mae held the bottle of vinegar in one hand and the loaf of bread under the other arm. Slowly, she inched across the plank, putting one foot carefully in front of the other.

Afterward, she wasn't sure what happened. Suddenly, her feet shot out from under her, and she splashed right into the cold water!

With one quick grab, she caught the plank and hung on with both arms. The current pulled at her.

Malinda's loaf of bread went bobbing along down the ditch, but the little bottle of vinegar sank out of sight.

Carefully, Mattie Mae pulled herself hand over

hand along the plank, and back to the bank. Here she
found a foothold in a muskrat hole along the side. Then
she reached up and grabbed a sapling. By pulling hard
with her arms and pushing hard with her knees, she got
out.

It seemed a long way back to the house, with her
wet clothes flapping about her. Mattie Mae was crying
when she burst into the kitchen, dripping puddles on
the floor. She was glad Mom was home.

"Why, Mattie Mae!" Mom exclaimed. "What happened?"

Everybody came running. Behind the cookstove,
Malinda helped Mattie Mae out of her wet clothes. She
rubbed her dry with a towel that Benjy brought. Then
Malinda helped Mattie Mae into her clean dry clothes
that Lizbet handed to her.

Becky made some boiling hot cocoa, and Ellie cut a thick slice of warm bread and put lots of butter and a big blob of honey on it.

"Now, tell us what happened," Mom said.

They all sat around the kitchen table and listened as Mattie Mae told her story. Benjy's eyes got bigger and bigger.

"We'll have to replace that plank with a footbridge, something wider, with rails along the side," Mom said. "I'm just so thankful that you lived to tell the story."

"What about adventure now?" Malinda asked. She explained to the rest, "Mattie Mae was worrying because nothing exciting ever happens to her."

Mattie Mae ate the last scrap of bread and drank the last gulp of cocoa. "Well, anyway," she said. "I guess this will be one story I can tell my children."

Then she leaned back and laughed with the others.

Topsy-Turvy Day

Mattie Mae sat on the side porch steps, feeling out of sorts with everybody, even herself. Usually, Saturday was lots of fun, but not this time. Mopsy was gone.

"How you can act like that over one cat is beyond me. After all, we have twenty-three others!" Malinda said.

"Mopsy is a special cat. She's my very own," Mattie Mae insisted.

She wished she could talk to Mom, but this was market day, so she was in town.

"Why don't you do something? Maybe she'll turn up by the time you finish," Malinda suggested.

"I've done all my chores. I've washed down the porch and scrubbed the steps and walk, clear out to the butcher house," Mattie Mae replied.

"Then go play with Lizbet and Benjy."

"I don't want to. They're both just babies. And Becky's reading, so she won't play with me." Mattie Mae kept feeling sorrier for herself by the minute.

Malinda's patience was giving out. "Then sit there and pout. I'm going to get dinner."

Dinner! Mattie Mae couldn't stand the thought. *How can anybody eat when Mopsy might be caught in a muskrat trap back along the big ditch somewhere? I don't think I'll ever be hungry again.*

When Malinda called her for dinner, she discovered that she felt hollow after all. Saturday dinner was always the same—a big kettle of potatoes, cooked in their jackets. One thing made it really special. The children could eat wherever they pleased. Once Mattie Mae had taken her plate to the orchard and climbed into an apple tree to eat!

Her favorite place was the front porch, though. Rover could lie at her feet, and once in awhile she'd snitch a bite for him.

"That dog will eat anything," Malinda sometimes said.

He wouldn't, though, Mattie Mae knew. She tried to give him an onion once, and Rover just turned up his nose.

Mattie Mae filled her plate with potatoes. She knew if she didn't take enough right away, she wouldn't get any more. The others liked them as much as she did.

She mashed the crumbly insides with a fork, added dots of butter and a spatter of salt, then poured creamy milk on top.

Rover lay on the ground, watching her as she squatted on the top step, holding her plate on her knees. She tossed Rover a bite, and he gulped it down whole. When he saw that he wouldn't get any more, he put his nose on his paws with a long sigh and began to doze again.

Mattie Mae ate the top layer first. It was so yummy that she forgot about Mopsy. Underneath, the potatoes weren't quite salty enough. With an eye on Rover, she slid her plate on the porch floor, out of his sight, behind a clump of pinks growing in the flowerbed. Then she sneaked into the house.

A minute later, when Mattie Mae came back with the salt shaker, her plate was gone.

"Benjy! Did you hide my plate for a joke?" she asked.

Benjy pushed the porch swing with one toe and shook his head. His mouth was so full of potatoes that he couldn't answer.

"Rover's gone, but he couldn't eat the plate. Oh, dear!" Mattie Mae wailed.

Malinda came running. "What in the world is it now, Mattie Mae?"

"My plate of potatoes. I left it right here—"

Malinda looked over the edge of the porch, among the pinks. There lay the plate, but it had already been licked clean.

"I'm sorry," she said. "Rover must have gotten your potatoes."

"Are there any left?"

"I'll look," Malinda promised.

The big iron kettle was empty.

"I'll fix you an egg—" Malinda began.

"Don't bother," Mattie Mae said stiffly. She was eight, going on nine, and too big to cry. It wasn't just the potatoes, of course! It was that, on top of all the worry about Mopsy—

"Where are you going?" Malinda asked.

"Outside."

Mattie Mae marched over to the orchard and then cut across to the catalpa grove. From there, she circled back to the barn and climbed up into the haymow. That ought to keep Benjy from trailing after her, for sure! She wanted to be alone.

For a long time, Mattie Mae just sat there, thinking. What a topsy-turvy day this Saturday had become! It was so quiet in the barn, with the sunbeams on the bright clean straw. She almost fell asleep.

Suddenly, plop! Something landed just beside her. It was Mopsy. She was purring to Mattie Mae like everything, too.

"Now, where did she come from?" Mattie Mae asked herself.

She climbed up where the hay was stacked high. In a little nest, close to the wall and warm and cozy, she

found two tiny kittens, their eyes tight shut.

Mopsy followed Mattie Mae to the nest and mewed anxiously.

"Don't worry. I won't hurt them," Mattie Mae promised. "A yellow one and one all striped, like its mamma. All the time I was thinking what an ugly day it was, and Mopsy was planning a surprise for me!"

Mopsy still seemed nervous, so Mattie Mae went away. She wouldn't come again until the kittens were older. She wouldn't tell Benjy and Lizbet right away, either, so they wouldn't bother them.

Suddenly, Mattie Mae had an idea. She'd call one kitten Topsy and the other Turvy! *Days* weren't topsy-turvy at all. It was only *people* who became that way. Maybe a little Topsy and a tiny Turvy would help her remember that.

"Mattie Mae! Mattie Mae!" Malinda called. She sounded worried.

"Coming!" Mattie Mae called back. Then she ran for the house as fast as she could go.

Good-bye, Uncle Tobe

"Mom, why didn't Uncle Tobe ever marry?" Mattie Mae asked.

Mom looked up from her sewing. "What made you think of that, Mattie Mae?"

"I don't know. I was just thinking about the stories he used to tell us. I wish he'd stay here all the time."

"So do I," Mom said.

Her voice had such a choked sound that Mattie Mae looked at her, hard.

"I haven't answered your question, have I?" Mom went on in such a cheerful tone that Mattie Mae wondered whether she had imagined the other sound. "Uncle Tobe had planned to marry a nice girl, but then the doctor told him he had a bad heart."

Mom took a couple of stitches, then stopped to stare into space. "Just about that time, Uncle Andy died."

"Who was Uncle Andy?" Mattie Mae asked.

"My, my! Such a question box! He was *our* uncle—Tobe's and mine. That would make him your great-uncle. Anyhow, Uncle Tobe saw what a hard time Aunt Rachel had in bringing up her children and keeping the farm going by herself."

"But what does all that have to do with Uncle Tobe not getting married?" Mattie Mae put in.

"Just give me time and I'll get to that. Uncle Andy's death made him think. He decided he wouldn't marry at all, since he knew he might not live to take care of his family, either."

"Ach, my! What about Uncle Tobe's poor girl-friend?" Becky asked. She had just come in, bringing the mail, with Lizbet trailing after her.

"She got over it in time, I guess. Anyway, she married somebody else."

"Well!" Becky said.

Mattie Mae knew Becky was thinking that it wasn't a bit like any of the stories she had read. Sometimes she would read some aloud to Mattie Mae, too. The stories were fun, but the people in them didn't act the way real people acted at all. Because of that, Mattie Mae always called them story people.

"Well, I'm glad he didn't marry," Lizbet said, "because he couldn't come to see us as often as he does if he had a family."

Then Ellie, Mattie Mae's next-to-oldest sister, banged into the room. She liked to bang around, "so

people know I'm busy," she sometimes said when Mom complained.

Ellie asked, "What came by mail, Becky?"

"Ach, here I'm forgetting to give it to Mom. And there's such a funny yellow envelope with it, too. It says Western Union."

Mom made a queer noise in her throat. Ellie turned white. "A telegram!" she gasped. "Oh, Mom! What is it?"

"Give me time to see," Mom said.

She sounded as if she was talking about any letter, but Mattie Mae noticed how her hands shook as she tore open the yellow envelope.

"It's Uncle Tobe," she said in a queer hushed voice. "He died yesterday."

For a minute, they were too stunned to say anything at all. Then Ellie put her hankie to her eyes and rushed out of the room. She almost bumped into four-year-old Benjy as she dashed through the doorway.

"What's the matter with Ellie, Mom? Is she mad about something?" Benjy asked.

"No, Benjy," Mom told him. She pulled him onto her lap. "We had a telegram telling us that Uncle Tobe went to heaven yesterday."

"Oh." Benjy looked a little puzzled. "Then he can't come to see us anymore? Not ever?"

Mom shook her head. Mattie Mae had to swallow something that kept coming up in her throat. *Uncle Tobe had loved us all so much!*

A minute later, she forgot all about her own feelings when Mom put her head down in her hand and began to cry.

Mattie Mae couldn't do a thing but stare. She had never really seen a grown-up cry before. And this was Mom, the person who always wiped away her children's tears and made them feel ever so much better. She and Lizbet and Becky looked at each other helplessly. Should somebody go out and tell Pop?

"If Uncle Tobe went to heaven, why are you crying, Mom?" Benjy asked.

Mom looked up quickly. "You remember how much we all missed Uncle Tobe when he left the last time?"

They all remembered. How empty and quiet the house had seemed after he was gone!

"Yet all the time we knew that he was back in Indiana, safe and sound, where he wanted to be, didn't we?"

Again, they all nodded.

"That still didn't keep us from missing him a whole lot. The same thing is true now. I know Uncle Tobe is in heaven, but I'll miss him just the same. He's my brother, you know."

"I see," Benjy said. He sounded so grown-up that Mattie Mae smiled to herself. "Thank you for explaining it to me, Mom."

Mattie Mae didn't say anything, but she felt just the way Benjy did. She was glad Mom had explained everything. She still felt sad because she knew that Uncle Tobe would never come back. But the queer feeling in her chest had disappeared.

I'm glad we've had an Uncle Tobe this long, Mattie Mae thought.

She hadn't told Mom what she was thinking about, but Mom smiled at her over Benjy's head, just as if she knew.

A Present for Cousin Lizbet

Pop drove Prince and the market wagon up to the house.

"All aboard!" he called.

He didn't have to call twice, either. Mattie Mae and Benjy and Lizbet and Becky and all the rest spilled out of the house and climbed through the doors at the back of the wagon. Mom climbed up and sat on the left side of the front seat, beside Pop.

"I can hardly wait," Mattie Mae said.

"Well, it's a long trip yet, so don't start bouncing right away," Mom told her.

Clip, clop! Clip, clop! Prince went down the highway. Mattie Mae looked out over Mom's shoulder. She could see Prince blow foam from his mouth in a long shuddering sigh every so often. She knew it was too soon, but she couldn't help looking around to see whether any sand dunes were in sight.

"Not for a long time, Mattie Mae," Mom said, just as if she knew exactly what Mattie Mae was looking for!

"I can't wait," Mattie Mae said again. "Cousin Lizbet and I are going to hunt all up and down the beach until we find a starfish. One with all the points on it."

Of all her cousins, Mattie Mae liked Lizbet best. It seemed like such a long time since she had seen her— not since the Sunday before last, on the church Sunday.

Mattie Mae's pop and mom belonged to the Amish Church. They all gathered for worship services every other Sunday, in the home of an Amish family. So this was an in-between Sunday, just right for a family outing.

"You're just lucky to be going to the beach," Mom told Mattie Mae. "Yonie Yoder's little Rachel has measles, and she was in church last Sunday. You children were all exposed to it."

"I hope we don't get it," Ellie said with a shudder. "Wouldn't that be awful if we were all in bed at the same time?"

"That's what happened when you had scarlet fever," Mom said with a sigh. "All of you had it, even Pop. I can tell you, I had my hands full."

Mattie Mae listened, but she didn't say anything. She kept looking ahead, because she wanted to be the first one to see the ocean. A long time later, they began going up the long rolling hills that were the sand dunes. A gull or two circled overhead.

It's close now, Mattie Mae thought as she hugged herself. *I can smell the saltwater.*

The air felt sticky hot in the market wagon, with its closed sides. But Mattie Mae knew how the breeze would feel against her cheek, in a minute, so fresh and sweet. That made her want to jump up and down. And the water!

They drove right down on the beach itself. Another market wagon stood not far away, and Grandpop came toward them.

"Did you hear about Cousin Lizbet, Mattie Mae?" he said. "She has the measles and couldn't come."

Grandpop lived right in the same yard with Cousin Lizbet, in a little house of his own.

"Ach, that's too bad," Mom said.

"I'll drive our market wagon over here and unhitch Prince," Pop said.

Mattie Mae hardly heard him. So Lizbet couldn't come! They couldn't hunt all up and down the beach for starfish, as they had planned to do together.

"This will be the girls' dressing room. The men will take the other market wagon for theirs," Pop explained.

Mom started pulling out bathing suits. Other aunts and uncles and cousins came up and began to talk. Mattie Mae and the other children got into bathing suits as fast as they could. They ran into the water, right in among the breakers. Frothy white tops broke over them. My, but it was fun!

If only Lizbet could be here, Mattie Mae thought.

After a bit, she walked down the beach. She was looking for starfish. Maybe—just maybe, she could find a perfect one by herself!

"Mattie Mae!" Mom called.

Mattie Mae ran back.

"You'll have to look out for Benjy."

"Ach, my!" Mattie Mae sighed. Then she took Benjy's hand, and they walked together, up the beach. "Look for the pretty starfish," she told him.

"Don't wanta look for a starfish! Wanta go in the water!" Benjy said.

She knew it wasn't any use to argue, so she went into the water with him. Benjy could be stubborn when he once made up his mind to do something. *Maybe later he'll go shell hunting with me,* she hoped.

Every time she tried to hunt for starfish and shells, Benjy shook his head.

"Wanta go in the water," he wailed.

After dinner, Mattie Mae suggested again, "Benjy, let's walk up the beach and look for a pretty starfish."

They started out, hand in hand. Mattie Mae found all kinds of shells, but no starfish. Some of them were tiny ones, pink on the inside and white along the edges. Some were big ones, with swirls, that you could hold to your ear after you got home. Then you could hear the roar of the waves all over again.

Lizbet might like to have one of those shells, while

she's in bed, Mattie Mae decided.

They walked and walked, picking up a few shells. "I don't see any starfish," Benjy said after a bit. "I wanta go in the water."

"You can't, Benjy," Mattie Mae explained patiently. "We've just eaten and will have to wait awhile."

Benjy paid no attention to her. He darted over and began to play in the breakers with his bare feet.

"Benjy! You come on out of there! The breakers are too big here," Mattie Mae called.

He just grinned and waded farther out.

Mom was too far away to call. Mattie Mae didn't know what to do. She ran after him, but Benjy just waded faster. Then she saw it, right there at her feet.

"Oh, Benjy! Look here!"

Benjy came running back. They both stared at the starfish lying there. Every point was perfect.

"Let's go and show it to Mom," Mattie Mae said.

Benjy ran ahead of Mattie Mae. He was as excited as she was.

"It's pretty," Mom said, taking the spiny starfish in her hand.

"Look, Grandpop," Mattie Mae said, holding it up for him to see.

"Yes, a starfish. It's too bad that Lizbet couldn't come today. She also wanted to find one."

Mattie Mae looked at her starfish for a minute. There wouldn't be a chance of finding another one, she was sure. She wanted this one herself. Then she thought of Cousin Lizbet, lying sick in bed instead of playing on the beach.

"Take it to Lizbet, will you, Grandpop?" She laid it in his hand. "And this big shell too. Maybe it will remind her about the sand dunes and the breakers and the gulls. I hope it will make her think about the sea all the time she's sick!"

"It might remind her about an especially nice cousin of hers, too," Grandpop said as he dropped the shells and the starfish into his pocket.

Where's Alice?

Mattie Mae ran out to the garden, where Mom was picking a long row of butter beans.

"Where's Alice, Mom?" she asked. Mom looked as if she didn't know who Mattie Mae was talking about.

"You know! The doll Aunt Mattie sent me in Benjy's box."

"The last I saw her, she was standing on her head in my sewing basket," said Mom.

"I remember! Cousin Lizbet and I had been playing—"

Mattie Mae was just ready to rush off to look when Mom stopped her.

"Help with these beans awhile, then you can go and look," she said. "It's hot out here, Mattie Mae, and my back aches from stooping."

So Mattie Mae stayed and helped Mom pick butter

beans. My, the rows seemed long! Her back ached too. Long before they were finished, she felt as if it would break in two any minute.

"You are such a big help, Mattie Mae!" Mom said as they carried the beans into the house.

Mattie Mae had a good feeling inside as she ran to look in Mom's sewing basket. There it was, on top of the sewing machine, but Alice wasn't standing on her head in it. She wasn't standing on her feet, either. Alice wasn't there at all.

So Mattie Mae ran out to the butcher house. Her big brother, Henry, was turning the sausage grinder. A long twist of meat curled out of it into a can below.

"Say, Mattie Mae, I'm so hot!" Henry said as he stopped to wipe his face.

Mattie Mae didn't even let him finish. She had a question she wanted to ask.

"Where's Alice?" she said. "You know, the doll Aunt Mattie sent me in Benjy's box."

Henry grinned and leaned closer. "The last I saw, her, she was out in the cow stable, pitching hay to the cows."

Of course, Mattie Mae knew he was just teasing. She laughed at the idea of Alice pitching hay with a big hay-fork.

"Bring me a drink, will you, Mattie Mae?" Henry asked as he went back to his sausage grinder.

Mattie Mae ran into the house. She pulled out some lemons and cut them the way Mom had showed her. She dumped just the right amount of sugar on top. Then she took the wooden potato masher and mashed them hard.

"Now, just *so* much water," she told herself.

She tasted a little and decided it would do. Henry's face looked bright when she came to the door of the butcher house with a pitcher and a glass.

"Pop will want some, too," he said. "He's in the washhouse, measuring out cottage cheese."

Mattie Mae took some lemonade to Pop in the washhouse. While he drank it, she asked, "Where's Alice, Pop? You know, the doll Aunt Mattie sent me in Benjy's box."

"Well!" Pop scratched his head. "Are you sure you didn't leave her in your playhouse in the catalpa grove?"

"I'll go look right now," Mattie Mae said.

She did hope she hadn't left Alice out there because it had rained last night. Rag dolls didn't like rain at all.

"Wait, Mattie Mae!" Pop said. "Malinda and Ellie would like some lemonade, too."

So Mattie Mae went out to the orchard. There, under an apple tree, her two oldest sisters were busy at a long table. They were dressing chickens.

"It's such work to get all these ready for market," Malinda said.

Ellie made a face. "I hate to dress chickens, too. It's such a smelly job."

Then they both saw Mattie Mae and the pitcher of lemonade. Their faces lighted up.

"Where's Alice? You know, the doll Aunt Mattie sent me in Benjy's box," Mattie Mae said as they gulped down their lemonade and held out their glasses for more.

"I saw her upstairs on the spare bed when I cleaned this week," Malinda told her.

"You were playing under the lilac bush with her yesterday," Ellie said.

Mattie Mae took the pitcher back into the house.

Now she had three places to look. She ran out to the catalpa grove first. Her playhouse was there, marked by strong strings stretched from tree to tree, making rooms. It smelled sweet because of the honeysuckle vines crawling up the twine and trailing everywhere.

The playhouse had a hidden, secret feeling about it because the brush and honeysuckles made high walls around it. The catalpa trees formed a speckled green roof high overhead.

Alice wasn't there, so Mattie Mae ran to the lilac bush. She crawled under it on her tummy, way, way back where she liked to go whenever she felt cross or tired or sad. Snow-on-the-mountain grew there, and she loved to look at the green and white leaves and stay in the cool shade until she felt happy again. Alice wasn't there either.

"Then I'll try the spare room," Mattie Mae muttered to herself. She climbed the stairs and opened the door. It had a musty, shut-up smell that made her wrinkle her nose. She was glad she didn't have to sleep on that bed with its high straw tick!

Still no Alice! Mattie Mae's feet dragged as she went downstairs. Just then Becky and Lizbet and Benjy returned. They had walked back to the swamp at the far end of their place to pick lilies.

"If we sell all of these at the market tomorrow, we'll have enough money to buy something nice," Becky said.

Mattie Mae didn't even smile. She didn't care how much money they would get. She wanted Alice, and that was all she wanted.

"Mom!" she called.

Mom was in the kitchen, putting supper on the table.

"What's the matter, Mattie Mae?" she said when she saw her daughter's face. "Benjy, you call the rest right away before everything gets cold."

"I can't find Alice, Mom. She just isn't anywhere," Mattie Mae wailed.

"Well, you helped me with the butter beans, so I'll help you hunt for her right after supper."

"And I'll help, too, because you were so good about bringing us some lemonade," Malinda said as she came in.

"Me, too," Ellie agreed.

When Pop and Henry heard that Alice was still missing, they said they'd help hunt, too. Of course, Becky and Lizbet and Benjy didn't want to be left out.

Right after supper, they all started out. They hunted in closets and under beds and in drawers.

Suddenly Henry yelled, "Here she is, Mattie Mae!"

Sure enough, there on the treadle of Mom's sewing machine lay Alice.

"She fell out of your sewing basket, Mom!" Mattie Mae gasped as she hugged Alice tight.

"I guess she got tired of standing on her head," Mom said.

"And to think that I never noticed!" Mattie Mae said.

"It takes a man to find things," Henry bragged.

Mattie Mae could tell he was teasing. She grinned right back at him.

"It takes a family, that's what it takes," she said.

Cousin Day

Mattie Mae jumped down from the buggy almost as soon as Mom said "Whoa!" Uncle Dave took Prince's bridle while the others climbed down.

Cousin Lizbet came running over. "Hurry up, Mattie Mae! We're playing Run, Sheep, Run."

"Not before she helps carry these things into the house," Mom said firmly.

Mattie Mae grabbed a bundle and dashed into the old farmhouse. At first, Uncle Dave's house had seemed funny to her, but she was used to it now. The house was built in the shape of a *T*, with the kitchen and storeroom in the stem. It had a porch all the way around it.

What seemed even stranger was Uncle Dave's whole place. It was right on the edge of the water—not the ocean itself, but an inlet. Mattie Mae could stand in the yard and see oyster boats out in the bay, and the long pier with water lapping gently against the piles.

Even the name of the place seemed funny: Witch Duck. Nobody seemed to know just why it had been called that, either.

Mom felt sorry for Aunt Mattie because Witch Duck was so far from all her relatives, with no bus nearby. That was one reason they had decided to have Cousin Day at Uncle Dave's that year.

The grown-ups didn't really call it Cousin Day. It was just that every summer all the aunts got together at one home or another. All day long they snipped and sewed and fitted. By evening most of the new school clothes would be finished—stiff denim pants and blue shirts for the boys, dresses and pinafores in green and blue and brown for the girls.

The children called it Cousin Day because they could play with their cousins all day long. Once in awhile, someone would have to go into the house to be fitted, but most of the time they could do whatever they wished.

Today, Cousin Lizbet took Mattie Mae outside with her. They played Run, Sheep, Run and Stoop Tag with the other cousins. Then they all walked down to the inlet.

The shore here wasn't nice and sandy, like the ocean beaches. Instead, it was full of reeds and tufts of grass. At one side, the marsh made a huge half circle of reeds, far into the land.

"Let's go over to the pier," Cousin Andy suggested.

"How would you get there?" Mattie Mae asked. To get to the pier, they'd have to cross the reedy half circle of marsh.

"We just run across on the piles," Yonie said.

For the first time, Mattie Mae noticed that there was a path of round posts right across the marsh. Once there had been a bridge on the piles, but now only the line of posts remained.

"You go across on *those?*" Cousin Lizbet sounded as if she couldn't believe it.

Mattie Mae didn't say anything. She liked the ocean, but this was different. Ever since her tumble into the big ditch at home, she was scared of water. She didn't want to say it because the rest might laugh, but she was afraid now.

"Look, it's easy," Yonie said. He skipped from one pile to the next, his bare feet never missing.

"But you live here, so you've had lots of practice,"

Cousin Lizbet said.

"Aw, come on! Let's go," Andy said. He was Yonie's brother, so he'd had plenty of practice, too.

One by one, the other cousins followed them. They didn't go as fast as Uncle Dave's children, but nobody fell in. Mattie Mae went last. She swallowed hard a couple of times, but she just *couldn't* tell the others that she was scared. She pretended that it didn't bother her at all.

Once on the other side, they ran down to the pier. The water kept slopping against the piles under the pier with a *whisp-whisp-whisp.* A gruff old man yelled at them to stay off, so they did. Yonie stuck out his tongue at him, but he knew the man was too far away to see him.

"Lizbet! Yoo-hoo-oo! Lizbet!" Lizbet's big sister, Annie, called. "Come, try on your dress."

They all started back with Lizbet. Yonie and Andy dashed across on the piles as quickly as before, but the rest just stood there.

Mattie Mae looked at the marshy water. She knew she couldn't bear to walk across it again. She just couldn't. Even if she was the only one who was scared, she decided not to pretend any longer.

"I'm scared," she said. "I'm going to walk out around."

"Me, too," Cousin Lizbet said.

"I was scared, coming over," Cousin Ada said. "But nobody else seemed to mind, so I didn't want to say

anything."

On the way back, Cousin Lizbet slid her arm into Mattie Mae's. "I'm glad you said that," she whispered. "It was a brave thing to do."

Then she ran off to have her dress fitted. The other children decided to play Pig in the Pen.

Mattie Mae stood in the yard, thinking. She had thought the others were brave, and they thought she was brave. Down underneath, they were all scared. Only Mattie Mae wasn't quite as scared now as she had been before.

"Come on, Mattie Mae!" Yonie called. So Mattie

Mae ran off to play with the rest.

The Happiest Girl in the World

Mattie Mae walked out to the highway in front of the house where the bus whooshed past on its way to town. Carefully she looked up and down the road. After she saw that no cars were in sight, she skipped across.

In the lane across the road, she slowed down and shifted the jug of lemonade she was carrying from one hand to the other. She was taking a drink to Pop and Henry, who were working in a field there.

Maybe I'll see her *today!* Mattie Mae thought.

Her was the little Baker girl. Mattie Mae didn't know her name, but she lived in the house at the end of the lane. Pop was such a good farmer that when Mr. Baker had bought the place several weeks before, he had come and asked him to farm their fields, too.

"They're unfriendly—those Bakers," insisted Mrs. Perry, who ran the little store on the corner.

Mattie Mae didn't think so. You didn't see much of them, that was true. But *she* always waved from their long black car as they slid past.

She must be the happiest girl in the world, Mattie Mae thought with a sigh.

Such lovely curls! Such frilly dresses, of soft colors like roses and daffodils and sweet peas. Mattie Mae looked down at her own plain Amish dress—brown, because that was a good dirt color. Mom and Malinda always had so much to do without more things to wash, and brown didn't look dirty so fast.

Mattie Mae's school dresses were purple and bright green or blue. Much better, of, course, but not as pretty as *hers*.

Best of all was the doll *she* sometimes held in her arms as they whizzed by. The doll had lovely curls, and her clothes were frilly and soft. The little dog was nice, too. He always barked at Mattie Mae, but not like he really meant it.

"Down, Jasper!" the little girl would say.

Mattie Mae shifted the lemonade jug again. Then she stopped and stared. A bit of pink showed through the tall grass in the ditch.

"What in the world! Why, it's *her* dolly!"

There she was, standing on her head among the weeds. Mattie Mae smoothed down the pink dress and brushed the rumpled curls with one hand. She wiped

the doll's eyes, nose and mouth.

"Mattie Mae Miller! Mattie Mae! Yoo hoo!" Henry yelled from the field where he and Pop were working.

"Coming!" Mattie Mae called back.

She pushed the doll back into the ditch and hurried on, across the flat field to Henry and Pop. All the land in that part of Virginia was flat.

Some places were too marshy to farm, like the swamp at the back of their own place. Or the big swamp that Mattie Mae had heard about, but never seen—the Dismal Swamp, to the south of them.

Pop sometimes talked about hills, but Mattie Mae couldn't imagine what they looked like. Today, as she shifted the heavy jug of lemonade from one hand to the other, she was glad their land was flat!

Mattie Mae shoved the jug into Pop's hands with a

74

quick message: "Mom says, 'Be sure to bring it with you when you come for supper.'"

Then she ran home as fast as she could.

"Mom! Mom! Guess what!" she gasped as soon as she got inside the kitchen.

Mom looked up with a smile. "You dropped the jug and broke it, so Pop and Henry didn't get a drop of lemonade."

Mattie Mae knew Mom was just teasing. When she told about the doll, Mom really did look surprised.

"You're sure it belongs to the Baker girl?" she said.

"Ach, yes. I've seen it often enough to know."

"Then you must take it back to her."

Mattie Mae stared. "She'll find it, won't she? I left it right there."

"It would be much kinder if you took it to their house."

Mattie Mae moved one bare toe along the pattern of the faded linoleum. "I'm—I'm kind of scared, Mom! "

"Why?"

"I—I won't know what to say. They're so different."

The Bakers weren't Amish, but that wasn't the only problem. Mattie Mae knew other "English" (non-Amish) people who didn't scare her a bit.

"They're—ach, well, you know what I mean, Mom!"

Mom nodded her head. "I know, but I still think you should take the doll over to their house. Wash your face, and I'll fix your hair—such a *schtrubbly* head! Put on your blue school dress."

"The new one? Oh, Mom! And may I wear my new school shoes, too? Please!"

"I don't care. If she asks you to stay and play, be sure to tell her mom you have to be home by five."

"I wouldn't want to even if she does ask me to stay," Mattie Mae said.

Mom shoved her off with a laugh, and she went upstairs to get ready. Becky and Lizbet and Benjy stood on the porch to wave good-bye. Mattie Mae wished one of them could go with her, but Mom said no.

Once more, Mattie Mae stopped and looked up the road. Then she looked down the road. She let a car whiz past before she skipped across.

The doll was still there, among the weeds. Mattie Mae picked her up and carried her carefully, in the crook of her arm.

A car! Beautiful frilly clothes! A doll like this! Surely *she* must be the happiest little girl in the world, Mattie Mae told herself as she went down the lane.

The house where the Bakers lived had been the big plantation house years ago when all the farms belonged to one family. Now they were owned by Pop and Uncle Alvin and Uncle Yonie—yes, even Perry down at the corner, and Troyer on the swamp road.

Like many of the old plantation houses, it stood in a big yard with the barn and other buildings. The front porch had high pillars. Mattie Mae looked up at the round window above her head. That was different from any window she'd ever seen. It was made of four red circles, four blue triangles, and a yellow square in the middle.

Mattie Mae clanged the bright brass knocker.

Her heart went *thump, thump!* Would the maid with her little cap, who sometimes came down the lane for the mail, open the door? Or Mrs. Baker, with her gray hair, in a lavender or dark blue dress? Or perhaps *she herself*—the little girl who owned the doll? Mattie Mae didn't know.

From somewhere inside, Jasper barked. Mattie Mae heard footsteps. They didn't sound like a little girl's footsteps, so she wasn't too surprised when Mrs. Baker herself opened the door.

"Why, you've found Serafina! Emily will be so happy," she exclaimed.

"Yes, ma'am," Mattie Mae said.

She never said *ma'am* to any of her Amish relatives and friends, but her schoolteacher had taught her to say it to the teacher. Mattie Mae sometimes used it with other people, too. She had to decide for herself just when to say it, but this seemed like the right time.

"What is it, Grandma?" a little-girl voice called.

"Just a minute, dear," Mrs. Baker called back.

Mattie Mae started to slip away, but Mrs. Baker put her hand on her arm.

"Don't go—please. Emily will want to see you.

She'll want to thank you for rescuing Serafina."

Mattie Mae had been finding things out by the minute. *Her* name was Emily. The doll was Serafina. And Mrs. Baker was Emily's grandmom, not her mom.

"Come," Mrs. Baker said, starting up the stairs. Mattie Mae followed her. Suddenly she stopped. There on the wall, just at the landing where the stairway turned, was a big flower with a yellow center and red petals. It glowed as if it were on fire.

"What—what is it?" Mattie Mae asked.

"What—oh, that. It comes from the round window. If you'll come on up, you can see."

Sure enough, Mrs. Baker was right. The sun shone through the colored glass so that the four red circles, the yellow center, and the blue triangles made a bright flower right on the wall.

"Hurry up, Grandma!" The voice sounded impatient now.

Mrs. Baker put her hand on Mattie Mae's arm. "She's been sick. That's what makes her fretful. You just bring Serafina right into the room. She'll be so surprised."

Emily was surprised. She sat straight up in bed.

"Oh, Grandma—it's Serafina! And she isn't hurt a bit. I lost her out of the car without noticing because Jasper made such a fuss, and we didn't know where to look."

"You're Mr. Miller's little girl, aren't you?" Mrs. Baker asked.

"Yes'm," Mattie Mae said in a whisper. It seemed so funny to hear Pop called *Mr. Miller* like that!

Mattie Mae looked down at the toes of her new school shoes. When she sneaked a glance, Emily was looking down at the foot of the bed as if she didn't know quite what to say, either.

"I'll get some juice and crackers, and you two can have a party up here," Mrs. Baker said.

She bustled out. Mattie Mae didn't know just how it happened, but in a few minutes she was curled up at the foot of Emily's bed, chattering away. Emily talked just as fast as she did. She showed Mattie Mae her books and her toys. So many and such bright new ones!

When Mrs. Baker came back, Mattie Mae remembered what Mom had told her.

"Oh, I almost forgot," she said. "Mom said I should tell your mom—"

Then she stopped and gulped. "Of course, she thought you were Emily's mom," she said to Mrs. Baker.

"I'm her grandma," Mrs. Baker said. "Emily doesn't have a mother."

"But Daddy comes as often as he can!" Emily said quickly.

Mattie Mae hardly heard her. *No mom! How—how awful that sounds!*

The orange juice tasted good. So did the crackers. Mattie Mae looked at everything, so she could remember to tell the rest at home—the pink wallpaper, with gray rabbits scattered all over it; the little rocker, just Emily's size; and the blue-and-white doll high chair.

Suddenly, a clock began to chime somewhere. *One—two—three—four—five strokes,* Mattie Mae counted.

She jumped up. "Mom said I should be home by five. I have to go right away."

"Come again, Mattie Mae!" Emily said. "Promise you will! Oh, it's been such fun!"

Mattie Mae looked at Mrs. Baker.

"Yes, do," Mrs. Baker said. "Emily's been sick, very sick. She's better, but the doctor says she'll have to be careful for a long time. I've been trying to find some nice quiet playmate for her, and I'm sure you'll be just right, Mattie Mae."

The red flower on the wall had climbed much higher when Mattie Mae went downstairs. She patted Jasper on the head as she hurried through the hall.

At the highway, she looked carefully both ways before she crossed. She was thinking hard, though.

Poor Emily! No mom, and she's sick and lonesome. That was so different from what Mattie Mae had imagined, that *she* must be so happy because of a doll and pretty dresses!

"Well, did anybody bite you?" Mom asked as Mattie Mae came in.

Mattie Mae knew Mom was teasing, so she laughed.

"Oh, Mom, they're nice. Really they are."

She went on to tell Mom and the others all about Emily.

"Of course you must go again," Mom said when she finished. "Here I was thinking the Bakers were kind of standoffish! You never can tell about people."

Mattie Mae nodded her head. She felt the same way. She skipped upstairs to change her clothes, feeling quiet inside.

She took off her new school dress and hung it in the closet. Then she sat on the floor and began to unlace her shoes. She was thinking hard.

Mattie Mae thought about the big house where the Bakers lived. She thought about the dolls and the lovely room and the doll high chair.

It would be nice to have things like that. She knew that. But would she really want to exchange that for their own house? It was old and weatherbeaten. It was much too small for all of them—Malinda, Henry, Ellie, Becky, Mattie Mae herself, Lizbet, Benjy, Mom, and Pop.

Mattie Mae jumped up suddenly and ran downstairs. "You know what, Mom?" she said. "I think I'm the happiest girl in the world."

Chrystobel

"Hurry up!" Mattie Mae's next-to-oldest sister, Ellie, called up the stairway.

"I *am* hurrying!" Mattie Mae called back.

She slipped on her bright blue going-to-town dress, added a long pinafore apron of the same color, then backed over to Becky to be buttoned up.

"She'll come soon," Becky called. "Where's your bonnet? Oh, here."

Mattie Mae grabbed the black bonnet and bounced downstairs. She and Ellie were going to town to take orders. Ellie went every week, but Mattie Mae did not often have a chance to go along.

"You keep poking along like this, and we'll miss the bus," Ellie warned.

Together they dashed out of the house. At the road, they turned to wave to Mom, who always watched from the window when her children were leaving.

Mattie Mae felt almost grown-up, standing there with Ellie. When the bus *whooshed* to a stop, she climbed on and found a seat while Ellie paid their fare.

She leaned against the window for a good look at their house, standing behind a tangle of shrubs—old and gray and tired-looking. No wonder! So many people tracked in and out all the time, their own big family, plus uncles and aunts and cousins of all sizes, to say nothing of neighbors and friends. Most of them were Amish, like Mattie Mae's own family.

There always seemed to be a lot going on, too—butchering pigs and chickens, cleaning and packing eggs, making cottage cheese, picking or pulling and bunching vegetables, all for the market and the route in town.

"We're busy, aren't we, Ellie?" Mattie Mae said.

Their house had whizzed out of sight already. How fast the bus went! Much faster than old Prince traveled when he took them to town in the market wagon, *clip-clop, clip-clop,* all the way.

"Too busy," Ellie said shortly.

"Do you like to go to town to take orders?" Mattie Mae asked.

"So-so." Ellie didn't sound as if she cared much. "It's better than butchering, any day."

Ellie made a face, almost as if she saw a dose of castor oil coming toward her. Mattie Mae didn't see why she should. Why, butchering was fun! Pop and Henry scraped off the stiff bristles. They cut and sawed and finally ran some of the meat through the grinder so that a long twist of sausage came out.

Malinda cleaned pigs' feet and helped stuff sausage. Mom cooked scrapple in a big iron kettle. She stirred the stiff, bubbly mush, then poured it into pans. Then Mom let Becky and Mattie Mae and Lizbet and Benjy scrape out the kettle, with its thick brown crust.

"Don't talk to me about butchering," Ellie said. "Just wait till you're old enough to do some of the messy jobs. You'll change your tune, too."

Ellie always talked in that sharp way. Mattie Mae didn't mind. Ellie was pretending to herself that she was as old as Mom instead of just fifteen.

When the bus pulled into the station in town, Ellie and Mattie Mae jumped out. Mattie Mae trudged along close beside Ellie because she was just a little afraid, even if she was eight years old. The town was so different from their own farm.

They climbed up steps to customers who lived in apartments four or five stories up. Then they came down, went to the next building, and climbed up again. How long some of the stairways seemed!

"You look tired, honey," one customer, Mrs. Endicott, said to Mattie Mae.

Mattie Mae looked down at her shoes. *Honey* was a word that made her feel bashful. Mom showed she liked them by a pat on the shoulder or something like that, never by calling them *honey*.

"Come in for just a minute," Mrs. Endicott said.

Ellie closed her order book and went, so Mattie Mae did too. They were in a long dining room with dark green blinds pulled down almost to the windowsill. Mrs. Endicott turned on the light.

"Ooo—ooh!" Mattie Mae said. There on the sideboard stood a dollhouse—like something out of a storybook. A little stairway went winding up through the hall. The twigs in the tiny fireplace glowed red. Everything was exactly the right size, too. It all matched the little house perfectly.

Best of all was a picture on the living-room wall of the baby Jesus and his mother. It was only postage-stamp size, but it had real glass and a carved frame.

Ellie touched Mattie Mae's hand. "We've got to go," she said. She didn't sound sharp this time, either, but as if she also would like to stay longer.

"It belonged to my daughter Chrystobel," Mrs. Endicott said, following them to the door. "She's married now and lives in Alaska. She was always so lively and cheerful! Never a cross word."

By then, Mrs. Endicott had talked them downstairs and out through the door to the street.

"Do you suppose Chrystobel was really as good as she says?" Mattie Mae asked. She couldn't quite believe in any little girl who *never* said a cross word!

Ellie shook her head. "I expect she was bad sometimes. But she acted nice most of the time, probably. So it's easy for her mom to forget the times she was bad."

By then they were climbing stairs again. They stopped outside a door on the third landing. Such a noise! Ellie had to knock three times before anybody answered.

When the door opened, the crying stopped for just a minute, then went on louder than ever. Mattie Mae could hardly believe her eyes. There on the floor lay a little girl about her own age, kicking and screaming like something wild.

"Well, she certainly wasn't any Chrystobel," Ellie said as they tramped downstairs again. High above their heads, they could still hear screams.

After that, they kept going from house to house. Some apartments were bright with new furniture and fresh paint. Others were gray and faded, with scuffed spots on the rugs and overstuffed chairs slumped in places from years of people sitting on them.

Some reminded Mattie Mae of her own home. Oh, they did have curtains at the windows instead of green blinds, like theirs. But there were toys scattered around, and children spilling over the floor. That made it seem like home, for sure.

"I never saw inside so many 'English' homes before," Mattie Mae said to Ellie on the way home.

Ellie didn't answer. Mattie Mae noticed that she was nodding off to sleep, so she propped her chin on her hands and stared out the window. She watched the houses whiz past, houses everywhere along the road.

They're all homes *for somebody,* she realized with surprise. She'd never really thought about it that way before.

Mattie Mae thought about their own house. It wasn't "fancy" because they were Amish. It wasn't new and bright because, with so many children, the money never seemed to go far enough. But Mom and Pop were kind.

They had good times together.

Nobody was quite as good as Chrystobel, of course, but nobody (not even four-year-old Benjy) lay on the floor and kicked and screamed, either.

Our house is a nice place, even if it's old, Mattie Mae thought. *That's because the people in it are nice.*

At that minute, their old gray house came into sight. Mattie Mae could see Benjy watching for them. She jabbed Ellie to wake her up. Then she reached for the bell cord and pulled it hard for the bus to stop. Yes, there were homes all along the highway, but this one was best of all.

Company for Mattie Mae

Mattie Mae liked having company. She liked to sit and listen to the grown-ups talk about long-ago times and retell old stories. Mom always shooed her away if they started telling any spooky stuff because she knew it scared Mattie Mae too much.

Company that came from far away was best. They always stayed overnight, and sometimes Mom forgot bedtime and let them all sit up a little later than usual.

"This company will have two little girls, just your age," Mom said when she told Mattie Mae who was coming.

"Two! Are they twins?"

"Ach, no. I told you before, but you didn't listen. There are two families coming. Dannie Jake's only have one child, so they are bringing her along. She's eight years old, just like you."

"And the other one?"

"That's Rufus Troyer's family. His wife is my cousin, too. They have a whole string of little ones, but they're only bringing Sarah and Joely, the baby."

"Oh, I can't wait! I just can't wait!" Mattie Mae clapped her hands and hopped up and down,

"Well, just remember, let the company play with your things. And play the games they want to play. Now mind!" Mom was particular about the way they treated company.

"Of course. I know that much."

"Yes, but you might forget. Especially if Nettie—" Mom caught herself suddenly. "Go and clean your shoes, Mattie Mae. They are a sight."

It seemed like a long time before the company came, but finally they arrived. At first, Nettie and Sarah just stood and looked at Mattie Mae, while Mattie Mae just stood and looked back at them.

"Go show them the kittens," Mom said.

Becky was playing with Joely. Benjy was listening to Pop and Jake and Rufus talk in the living room.

"Take Lizbet with you," Mom said as they started out.

The barn was warm and nice in spite of the cold outside. Topsy and Turvy were tumbling over the hay, and it wasn't long until all three girls were chattering as fast as they could.

"We have a puppy at home," Sarah said. "I wish you could see him. He acts so cute sometimes."

"I have six dolls," Nettie announced.

Mattie Mae stared at her. Six dolls! She'd never heard of anybody having so many.

"That's right," Sarah said. "They live close to us, so I've seen them. One is so big."

She measured with her hands. Lizbet opened her eyes wide and her mouth became a big *O*. Mattie Mae felt the same way, although she didn't show it quite as much.

"I have lots of other toys, too," Nettie went on. You could tell she felt important. "A doll high chair and a cradle. And, oh, ever so many others."

"Did—didn't you bring any of them with you?" Mattie Mae asked.

Nettie looked down at the toes of her shiny new shoes. She scuffed up the hay with one foot.

"Ye-es, I did. But—" Her voice trailed away.

Mattie Mae couldn't understand why she acted like that. Suddenly, Nettie leaned over close to her.

"I'll show it to you if you get rid of Lizbet," she whispered behind her hand.

"Well, I can try." Mattie Mae sounded doubtful. Lizbet could be as sticky as flypaper when she wanted to be around. If she knew they were trying to get rid of her, she'd just be that much worse.

"Go and ask your mom if we can have some cookies," Nettie said.

As soon as Lizbet went, she grabbed the other girls' hands. "Come on! Let's go."

Mattie Mae thought it seemed like a mean trick, but she couldn't tell company that. She ran to the front door with Nettie and Sarah, and they sneaked upstairs without anyone knowing it.

"Here," Nettie said. She pulled out a suitcase and opened it. "See!"

She held up a little toy washing machine. It looked just like a big one, but this was only about six inches high.

"If you turn this crank, it makes the washer go. And if you turn this one, the wringer goes around," Nettie explained.

"Oh, let me see it," Mattie Mae said.

Nettie pulled back. "Nobody else is supposed to touch this at all," she said. "You might break something."

Mattie Mae's hand dropped. Sarah moved over and stood close beside her.

Nettie looked at them both. "We could try it out. Don't you have a place we could go, where Lizbet wouldn't see us?"

Mattie Mae swallowed hard. Then she nodded. After all, even if Nettie was selfish, she was still company. And Mom always said you did what company wanted to do.

"Well, if the rest of us daren't touch it, you can just put your washing machine away," Sarah said, sharply.

Nettie stared for a minute. Then Sarah went on.

"If you'd rather, you can go ahead and play with it

by yourself. Mattie Mae and I are going to do something that's more fun than watching you show off."

She grabbed Mattie Mae's hand and started downstairs. "She's a selfish thing," she whispered in Mattie Mae's ear.

In a minute, Nettie was with them. "I don't want to play by myself. I want to do what you girls do."

Mattie Mae looked at her. She felt a little sorry for Nettie. Being selfish couldn't be much fun, because that way nobody wanted to play with you.

"Let's go get Lizbet and play house," Mattie Mae said. "We can take our dolls, and Lizbet can be the little girl."

"I want to be the mom," Nettie said quickly.

"All right." To Mattie Mae's surprise, Sarah gave in right away. Maybe she didn't want to fuss all the time, either. "I'll be the pop, then."

"And I can be the grandmom," Mattie Mae said. "Mom will let me have her shawl and that old bonnet she wears when she picks berries in the summer."

They raced off together. *Company's fun,* Mattie Mae thought to herself. Then she remembered how Nettie had acted. *Anyway, some company is fun.*

Mattie Mae squeezed Sarah's hand hard. Then she ran to ask Mom for the bonnet and shawl.

Namesakes

Mattie Mae and a crowd of sisters and cousins, from eight to eighteen years old, sat in Aunt Amanda's living room. They were waiting for her to tell them why she had asked them to come.

"I've got a little job for you," Aunt Amanda explained.

She was the youngest and prettiest of all Mattie Mae's aunts. When she married Uncle Yonie, over a year ago, she moved to a farm not far from Mattie Mae's own home.

"See, here are patchwork pieces, a dozen of them altogether. It's a kind of patchwork called appliqué."

Appliqué! Mattie Mae tried the new word on her tongue, but it didn't seem to fit at all.

"I don't know how to do that," she said.

She had learned about patchwork long ago, but this

was different. Aunt Amanda had a white block with a picture printed on it, rabbits and puppies and kittens. Then she had a stack of colored patches.

"Isn't she the dumbhead, though?" Cousin Mattie was whispering behind her hand to Lydia, but Mattie Mae heard it anyway. She didn't like Cousin Mattie, even if they both had Grandmom's name and Aunt Mattie's name. She always acted so hateful.

"Some people think they're so smart," Cousin Lizbet whispered to Mattie Mae.

She said it loud enough for Cousin Mattie to hear on purpose, though. Cousin Mattie turned red.

Aunt Amanda went on as if she didn't notice anything. "I know some of you have never done this before, but I'll show you how."

Aunt Amanda took a needle and showed them the little over-and-over stitches that held the bright patches in place. But Cousin Mattie wouldn't even look.

"My mom showed me that long ago. I'm not a *baby.*"

She looked across at Mattie Mae. Cousin Mattie was really only two months older than Mattie Mae, but she always acted as if she knew everything.

"If you each do one patch, I'll have enough for a quilt," Aunt Amanda went on.

"Twelve patches isn't enough," Cousin Lizbet said.

Mattie Mae nodded her head in agreement. She knew that much about patchwork quilts. She had seen Mom lay out rows and rows of patches on the bed before she had enough for a whole quilt.

Aunt Amanda just laughed. "It will be enough for this quilt."

"You haven't told us who it's for," Mattie Mae's sister Malinda said. She said it in a joking way, but Mattie Mae really did wonder.

"You'll find out someday!" Aunt Amanda said, as she started handing out blocks and patches.

"Look!" Ellie said. "I have a blue puppy for my block."

Aunt Amanda looked at the patch Ellie was holding. "Yes! I had a dress like that when I was eleven, just Becky's age. Grandmom made it for me."

"Tell us about Grandmom," Becky said.

The cousins all liked to hear about Grandmom. Some of them remembered her, of course, but Mattie Mae didn't. She was only a baby when Grandmom died. Mattie Mae liked to hear about her because she was her namesake.

"There never was anybody else like her," Amanda said slowly. "She was always so jolly and kind. Nothing ever made her cross. Not even the time I tipped over the churn and spilled a whole lot of cream right on the floor. She helped clean the mess away and even laughed while she was doing it."

"I wish I could have known her," Cousin Lizbet said.

Aunt Amanda looked around the room. "Anybody who has her name has a lot to live up to," she said.

At that minute, Mattie Mae looked across at Cousin Mattie. She was sewing a red lamb on her patch, but she wasn't using the over-and-over stitches Aunt Amanda had shown them. Instead, she was sewing around the edge with just ordinary stitches.

Here was Mattie Mae's chance to get even with Cousin Mattie for all her meanness.

Mattie Mae had already opened her mouth to say something smart, but she closed it again before a word slipped out. Grandmom! Aunt Amanda had said anybody who had her name would have a hard time living up to it. And Mattie Mae knew that Grandmom would never, *never* have made fun of someone else's mistakes.

Instead of saying something to make them all laugh

at Cousin Mattie, Mattie Mae edged around to Aunt Amanda's side. She nudged her and nodded toward Cousin Mattie's block.

Aunt Amanda got up right away. "If you work so hard, I'll have to feed you, I guess. Cousin Mattie, would you like to help me in the kitchen for a bit?"

Nobody but Mattie Mae noticed that when Cousin Mattie laid down her quilt block, Aunt Amanda slipped it into her apron pocket.

She'll explain it out in the kitchen, Mattie Mae thought. *That way the rest won't know.*

She felt so good inside that she started humming a little tune as she stitched over and over around the edge of her purple kitten.

She felt still better, about two months later, when Mom told her she could go to Aunt Amanda's again.

"You and Becky can go. Aunt Amanda has a surprise over there for you," Mom said.

Mattie Mae was so excited that she could hardly wait. As soon as she got inside the front door, she heard the surprise right away.

"A baby! You have a baby, Aunt Amanda," she said as she dashed into the bedroom.

"Ach—not so loud now!" Aunt Ada warned. She was Aunt Amanda's nurse.

Aunt Amanda didn't seem to mind the noise.

"Come, look at your new cousin," she said. "And Mattie Mae, just guess what her name is!"

"Amanda, maybe?"

"Ach, no!" Aunt Ada said.

They were all looking at her and laughing. Suddenly, Mattie Mae knew.

"Grandmom has another namesake!" she said.

"That's right. This is little Mattie." Aunt Amanda looked so happy as she smoothed the baby's bright blue dress.

Becky begged to hold the baby, so Aunt Ada let her do that for just a minute.

"She's also Aunt Mattie's namesake and your namesake, too, Mattie Mae," Aunt Amanda said softly. She smiled up at Mattie Mae. "Don't you think she has a lot to live up to, though?"

Mattie Mae could feel herself turning red, but she liked it just the same. She knew Aunt Amanda was remembering that day when they were sewing quilt patches. There on the baby's bed lay the quilt with Ellie's blue puppy, Cousin Mattie's red lamb, and Mattie Mae's own purple kitten.

She stooped and touched baby Mattie's soft little fist carefully. *Oh, it is so nice to have a new little cousin named for me,* she thought.

"We'll both have a hard time living up to Grandmom," she told Aunt Amanda happily.

The Christmas Closet

Christmas! Mattie Mae gave a hop and a skip down the walk.

"Only three days away, too!" she told Rover.

Rover wagged his tail just as if he understood every word she said. So Mattie Mae went on.

"Our house is so full of secrets, I'm afraid it's going to pop wide open one of these days. Ach, my! There's a closetful of secrets upstairs right this minute, Rover!"

Just then the big blue bus *whooshed* to a stop out front. Mattie Mae's mom and her Aunt Ada got out.

Mattie Mae almost fell over Rover as she dashed toward them. Her little sister, Lizbet, and little brother, Benjy, came running out as fast as they could.

"Let me carry your shopping bag, Mom," Mattie Mae said.

"No, let me!" Lizbet shouted.

"I want to! I want to!" Benjy screamed.

"Children!" Mom said sharply.

Mattie Mae knew she was ashamed because of Aunt Ada. She didn't have to be, though. Aunt Ada's children (mostly boys) acted just as bad or worse. And that shopping bag looked so interesting, bulging with packages.

"I'll carry it myself," Mom said. "Now, it's no use sticking your long nose this way, Benjy. You won't get to see those presents till Christmas anyway."

"I have such a time with my little snoopers, too," Aunt Ada said with a sigh. "I hardly know where to hide the presents anymore."

"We keep ours in a closet upstairs," Mom said. "One with a lock and key, of course!"

Mom and Aunt Ada laughed. They went into the kitchen, where Malinda and Ellie were baking cookies and frying doughnuts.

"That's what we're supposed to bring to Grandpop's for the Christmas dinner," Mom explained.

The kitchen smelled so good that Mattie Mae's mouth watered. Benjy slipped up to the table. He looked at the heaps of brown raisin cookies. So many! Mattie Mae knew he was thinking, *Ellie won't miss just one.* His hand slid over toward the stack.

"Now none of that!" Ellie said sharply.

She gave Benjy's hand a smack, but when Mom frowned at her, she let him go.

"Mattie Mae," Mom said. She was taking off her

shawl and bonnet now. "Here, put this package on the table. It's a tablecloth. The rest is all Christmas stuff. Better take it up to the closet right away. I'll get the key for you."

Mom started toward the living room. "You come, too, Ada. I want to show you that new quilt pattern Aunt Mattie sent me. I think I'll try that one next."

Mattie Mae shivered because the living room was so cold. They had a stove in it, but it cost too much to keep a fire going all the time. Mom started it every Sunday and when she knew company was coming, but that was all. In the evenings, their own family usually sat in their large farmhouse kitchen, where the cookstove kept them warm.

"Here, Mattie Mae," Mom said. She took the key from its high nail and dropped it in her hand. "Now, look at this, Ada—"

Mattie Mae didn't stay to hear any more. She ran upstairs, with the shopping bag going *bump, bump, bump* against her leg at every step.

The room where the presents were kept was right above the living room. Through the air register, Mattie Mae could hear Mom and Aunt Ada talking about quilts as she unlocked the closet door.

My, how interesting it looks! she thought. The box Aunt Mattie had sent stood on the floor. Another shopping bag hung on a hook, and the shelf was crowded with boxes.

Mattie Mae looked around. She looked down at the

shopping bag in her hand. *Surely one little peek won't hurt! Besides, no one would ever know.*

Just then, she heard Aunt Ada say, "I'm surprised you let Mattie Mae take that key by herself, Lizzie. Are you sure she won't snoop?"

"I don't think so," Mom said. "Mattie Mae behaves well, for an eight-year-old. I'm surprised at her sometimes. At her age, I used to be such a *Schussel* (scatter-brain) myself."

They laughed together again. Mattie Mae didn't laugh, though. Instead, she shoved the shopping bag into the closet and locked the door again, right away. Then she took the key down to Mom.

All the children, from eleven-year-old Becky on down, got up early on Christmas morning. Their plates were still on the dining-room table, just where they'd put them the evening before. Now they weren't empty anymore.

"Oh! Oh, Mom!" Mattie Mae said when she saw hers.

On the plate stood a little doll bed about six inches long. It had a tiny pillow, sheets, and even a real quilt! And in it was the smallest rag doll Mattie Mae had ever seen.

"Isn't she sweet?" Mattie Mae said.

"I think so, too," Becky agreed. "Mom and Malinda and Ellie and I worked awfully hard finishing the doll, the bed clothes, and stuff."

"I'm going to call her Carol," Mattie Mae said.

"That's a good name for a Christmas baby." She was her first doll not named Alice.

"Did you guess what we were giving you?" Becky asked.

"No." Mattie Mae shook her head. "I could have snooped and found out, when Mom brought it home. But, oh, Becky, it's much more fun being surprised."

Mattie Mae laid Carol back in her little crib. Yes, being surprised was more fun, but having Mom trust her was even better.

"I'm going to take you along to Grandpop's to show Cousin Lizbet," Mattie Mae told Carol.

The whole day lay ahead—fun with Cousin Lizbet, seeing Grandpop and Aunt Gertie and all the other relatives, and hearing the grown-ups talk about old times. Mattie Mae was glad she hadn't spoiled any of it by snooping.

"Christmas!" Mattie Mae hopped up and down. "Isn't it the nicest time of the whole year?" she asked.

Becky and Lizbet and Benjy were too busy playing with their own presents to answer her.

THE AUTHOR

Edna Beiler began her career as a freelance writer, providing stories and articles for various ages in Sunday school papers. Her first book, *Ten of a Kind,* was published in 1953. Since then she has written *Adventures with the Buttonwoods; Mitsy Buttonwood; Tres Casas, Tres Familias; White Elephant for Sale;* and *Mattie Mae,* which has more than 20,000 copies in print.

For seven years Beiler served on the staff of Mennonite Board of Missions as a writer and editor. During that time, she wrote three missions studies for children and served as editor of the Voluntary Service publication, *Agape.*

She has attended Arizona State University, Indiana University, and Goshen College. Before her retirement in 1988, she served ten years as a caseworker for the Hancock County (Indiana) Welfare Department and worked as a social worker for the Indiana State Welfare Department for another ten years.

Edna Beiler resides in the Indianapolis area and attends St. Matthew's Church.